THE CONSCIENCE
OF THE KING

THE CONSCIENCE OF THE KING

A NOVELLA BY

PERRY SLAUGHTER

SINISTER REGARD
New York
2015

ISBN 978-1-941-92845-5

Trade paperback edition: July 2015

www.sinisterregard.com
www.perryslaughter.com

For the Bard, once more

THE CONSCIENCE OF THE KING

I.

BERT DRAM STOPPED TO CATCH HIS BREATH, LEANING FORWARD with his hamlike hands braced on his knees. "We should go back," he said between gasps. The sun was hidden by malevolent yellow-gray clouds, but still the sweat poured down his face and back. His lungs burned. "There's an evil magic all over this country. It's is not a place for us, Jacques."

Jacques turned on the hard-packed road, wandered back a few paces, and peered at Bert with a strange look in his green eyes. "If I didn't know you better, Bert," he said, "I'd think you were saying this is no place for *you*."

"It's no place for *any* of us," Bert said with all the force he could muster. He straightened up and motioned for the wagon a dozen paces behind them to stop. The other members of the troupe murmured and grumbled, but kept their respectful distance. As the creaking of the wheels faded and the two aging horses began to stamp and champ wearily, Bert gestured at the landscape all around them. "Just look. It's taking something out of us simply to *be* here."

The land to either side of them was caked dry and studded

with stunted scrub for as far as the eye could see. Behind them it was all the same, save for the occasional small village or solitary dirt hovel that seemed on the edge of drying up and blowing away in the hot wind. Thirty leagues back, the horizon held a hint of greenery, but in the days since they had entered the land of Montravel, Bert had forgotten what a living, breathing tree looked, smelled, and felt like. The people they had encountered along the way moved listlessly, despite their thickset builds and sturdy limbs. Their eyes were dull, and their mouths frozen in creased frowns. An impromptu performance in the first village the troupe passed through had elicited nothing but curious glances and deepened frowns. They had not tried performing in public since.

But the worst leagues lay ahead, up the slight rise that seemed to grow steeper with every step. The landscape before them seemed even more barren and blasted than what they had already passed through, and far in the distance, at the summit of a rocky promontory that looked out over unimaginable wastes, their final destination awaited them, half-shrouded in the murky, almost luminescent clouds that never seemed to disperse, an upthrust fist of dark stone that stood as both a warning and a challenge to the skies.

Montravel Keep. Bert felt a stony fist inside his stomach every time he raised his eyes to it. In all his sixty years, he had never experienced such raw dread as he did now, regarding the castle. He had to look away.

This was magic of the worst sort. It radiated from the Keep, seeped like infection into the land itself. Bert mistrusted magic at best, feared it at worst, but this was magic of a maleficence orders beyond any he had encountered before.

Something terrible would happen in that castle, he knew.

Something terrible *had* happened there. Bert did not want to learn what.

Jacques's gaze traveled around the landscape with Bert's, then settled, hard as iron, on Bert's face. "It's just the slope, Bert," he said. His voice was not loud, but there was a harsh edge to it that Bert had never heard before. "It's so long that you don't realize how steeply you're climbing. It throws your perspective off." He shrugged. "It's a place, like any other."

Their eyes remained locked for several seconds before Bert finally looked away. Bert wanted to ask Jacques why he was lying, but held his tongue. He had known and trusted Jacques for over fifteen years. He knew there was a reason for every odd decision Jacques made.

But traveling to Montravel Keep for a command performance before King Philip the Good was the oddest decision of them all.

Bert looked at Jacques again, but Jacques was gazing toward the distant castle. His expression was unreadable. Jacques was tall and powerfully built, his muscles lithe from decades of dancing. He wore his jet-black hair long, and his beard, though very short, was the same dense and impenetrable black. When Jacques had been a mere twenty, he had hired Bert as propmaster for his band of traveling actors and acrobats. They had crisscrossed two continents together in the time since, and Bert presumed that he knew Jacques as well as any man alive did. There had always been a strange, buried hardness about Jacques, but it was now closer to the surface than Bert had ever seen it. He did not like seeing it. He was afraid of what it might conceal.

"So, we continue," Jacques said, turning back to Bert. "It's mid-morning now. If we keep up this pace, we'll arrive at the Keep before we've lost the sun."

"Respectfully, Jacques," Bert said, "we lost the sun the moment we set foot in this godforsaken country."

Jacques clapped Bert on the shoulder, but there was neither warmth nor mirth in his smile. "Keep that sense of humor, Bert," he said quietly. "We're going to need it, unless I miss my mark."

The horses whinnied, and Bert turned to see that young Emile had crossed half the distance from the wagon to where he and Jacques were standing. "What is it, Emile?" Bert asked, somewhat more harshly than he had intended.

Emile was a young, thin boy with lanky brown hair. He took part in a few of the scenarios that required the full complement of players, but other than that, his job was to look after the horses. He had a small magic talent—an uncanny facility with animals—but Bert liked the boy despite that. Magic talent was rare, and Emile did his job well. He was never obtrusive or arrogant about his ability. He used it only when necessary, but still Bert kept a wary eye on him. Emile had been with the troupe only six moons. Bert was not exactly suspicious of the boy—he was merely exercising caution.

The only other member of the troupe with any pretensions to magic talent was Claude Villy, but Bert knew Claude's claims were false. The man could conjure the strangest things out of thin air—such as coneys and corset bones, orchids and orioles—but it was all legerdemain. His was an act designed to delight crowds, and no one took it seriously.

Emile ducked his head and wrung his hands. "It's Beetle and Brow, sir," he said. He seemed pained by what he had to say. "I'm not sure how much longer they can keep this up. They're all a-lather, and there's hardly any water left for them, and now they're starting to foam . . ."

Bert sighed and ran his hand over the white stubble on his

head. He looked back and forth between Jacques and the horses.

"Tend to it, Bert," Jacques said, his mouth tight. "I suppose we can afford a brief rest before continuing."

Bert nodded, then trotted back downslope with Emile toward the wagon and the ten other members of the troupe. He glanced over his shoulder at Jacques only once. Jacques stood like a statue, hands on his hips, gazing at Montravel Keep with an intensity that burned like slow fire.

What on earth does he see up there? Bert wondered. Why has he dragged us into this hell?

"The foaming started maybe half an hour ago," Emile was saying as they approached the horses. "Just a little at first, but it's steadily gotten worse. I wasn't too concerned before, but now they're at rest and it hasn't gotten any better. I can't seem to help them . . ."

Bert collected himself enough start examining the horses. He touched the thick white foam at the corner of Beetle's mouth, though the old mare shied away from his hand and tried to rear up in her yoke. As Bert sniffed the foam, the other players closed in around them.

"Sardin' bad business, this," said Guillaume Roe, the group's best physical comedian. He scratched at his curly, grizzled hair. "Can't you talk some bloody sense into him, Bert?"

Several others murmured their agreement.

Bert wiped his hand on his trousers while Emile tried to calm the horses. "Jacques says we continue, so we continue." He turned, giving the men his best steely glare. "Anyone have a problem with that?"

Eyes fell. "*I* got a sardin' problem," Guillaume said, but his voice lacked conviction.

"Then get over it, Guy," Bert said. "This is an important engagement." He didn't add that he had no idea why. "Now, we've got a rest for a few minutes while we work with the horses, so take advantage of it. Come on. Scatter!"

The men shambled away listlessly as Bert turned back to the horses. He felt guilty about taking such a hard line with the troupe, but it was necessary. He saw the way the fire had leaked out of them over the past days. They were only shadows of the men he had worked beside for so long.

Bert circled around Emile and ran a hand down Brow's flank. Her sweat was sticky and foamlike. Her eyes rolled haphazardly in their sockets, and she snorted and whickered in a peremptory way.

"I've never seen them like this," Emile said, after his soothing noises had failed to calm the horses.

"Well, they're certainly exhausted," Bert said. "And after only a few hours of travel. But what else is wrong with them?"

Emile shook his head. "I think they're afraid, Bert," he said. He looked at the other men, some of them flopped down in heaps in the road, some of them huddled together in small groups, then lowered his voice. "Frankly, so am I. And I don't know why."

"It's the climb, nothing more," Bert said, though he could not meet the boy's eyes as he did.

"It's more than that," Emile said. "I know you don't like hearing about things like this, but I've tried everything I know to get the horses moving, right up to conjuring the scent of fresh water ahead. I don't like doing that, because it's like lying to them, but it always works. Always until now."

Bert shook his head. "We're going to have to lighten the load, that's all. The rest of us are going to have to help port the gear."

He strode around the side of the wagon without waiting to hear Emile's reply. Fading paint on the weathered wood proclaimed, in red, yellow, and blue letters:

JACQUES PAINE & THE PAINE PLAYERS

World-Renowned! Performers for Kings! Delight of Queens!

Comedy · Music · Tragedy · Acrobatics · Magic · Grand Guignol

As Bert unlatched the fold-down panel, he sensed a presence at his shoulder, though he had heard no one approach. Startled, he turned to find himself facing Rene Lyons, a lean man with ragged blond hair and a scar that ran beneath one eye and over the bridge of his nose. "You scared me, Rene," Bert said, though the truth was that Rene *always* scared him.

"We're not stopping here," Rene said. His voice was flat, affectless, and the words were neither question nor statement.

Rene had joined the troupe a couple of years earlier, and Bert had always debated the wisdom of his hiring. Rene was only a fair actor and could not dance at all, but he was like lightning with a sword, and his flourishes in fight scenes consistently brought audiences to their feet. Still, Bert had never felt quite right about Rene. He was too aloof, too withdrawn, and he nursed an inherent meanness that seemed likely to erupt into violence at any moment. It hadn't happened yet, but Bert knew it was only a matter of time until it did.

But Rene was somehow a friend of Jacques's, so Bert went along with it. Jacques had never hired a man without reason— even if he never divulged those reasons.

"Like I told everyone a minute ago," Bert said, rubbing his chest where his heart hammered like a racing stallion, "this is just a brief rest. We'll get going as soon as we unload some things.

Everyone's going to have to carry something. In fact, why don't you round everyone up so we can get started."

Rene drilled Bert with his gaze for a moment, but Bert held his ground. Rene turned without a word and drifted toward the nearest knot of men.

There were loud groans of protest, but before long something had been unloaded for every man to carry. Even Jacques returned to the wagon and left with a bag of wooden swords, knives, and pistols slung over his shoulder. Bert tried to see that every man was given something scaled to his own strength, and he saved the heavy chest of costumes for himself and Guillaume to lug together. Emile received the lightest bundle, a sack full of cookware.

"Are we ready now?" Bert asked, surveying the laden troupe.

The men murmured their assent, and Bert gave the order to move out.

Jacques started up the road ahead of everyone else, but the horses would not move. They shrank back in fear, whinnying and tossing their heads, as Emile tried to yank them forward by the reins.

"Come on, damn it all," Bert said, feeling his stomach tie itself into knots even as he and Guillaume hoisted the costume chest between them. "We have time to make up."

"I'm trying," Emile said, his face red with exertion or embarrassment or both. "I'm trying."

"Looks like these horses is the only ones of us with any sardin' sense," Guillaume said, setting down his end of the chest. "Looks like we're staying here after all."

Jacques came striding back, and Bert could see the lines of strain around his mouth as he tried to control his impatience. "What's the problem now?"

"Horses, sir," Emile said. "They—they're not cooperating."

"Make them," Jacques said, turning back up the road. "We need to move."

Bert set down his own end of the chest. "Loosen up the reins, Emile," he said, then carefully approached Beetle and placed a flat hand on her shoulder. She seemed to shrink down into herself at his touch, but did not resist. Her muscles were trembling so severely that Bert's hand tingled. He shook his head. "Jacques, these horses aren't going anywhere. They're worn right out."

Jacques stopped his resolute march up the road, but he did not turn. "Then we leave them," he said in a voice taut with self-control. "Everyone carry what you have and follow."

Bert felt a sudden exhaustion of his own wash over him, even as a cold chill stole up his back. Wiping the thick horsesweat from his hand, he hurried to where Jacques stood. He stopped a pace back, to the man's right. "Jacques," he said quietly, trying to banish the note of pleading he heard in his own voice, "you can't be serious. This place is draining us all. Look what it's done to the horses. We'll *all* be like that by afternoon, some of the men even sooner."

Jacques stood silently, as if defying Bert to continue.

Bert shook his head. "And even if we make it to the castle," he said, "what makes you think we'll be in any shape to perform?"

"It won't be a problem," Jacques said, never taking his eyes from the castle.

Bert's shoulders slumped. The way he felt, he wanted to drop to the ground and never get up again. "I don't get this, Jacques," he said in a defeated voice. "I really don't get this."

"You don't need to. You only need to follow my orders."

"You're orders are going to kill us."

Jacques's head snapped suddenly to the right. His eyes burned more fiercely than Bert had ever seen them. "We *will* reach the Keep by evening," he said in a sharp, soft hiss, "and we *will* perform for the king. I've spent too many years trying to arrange this to quit now."

Bert took a step back, as if recoiling from a striking viper. He'd had no notion until two weeks before that Jacques had ever in his life entertained hopes of performing in Montravel. It made no sense, no sense at all. "This land is cursed, Jacques," he said quietly.

Jacques nodded, at last allowing a bit of his own weariness to show. "Aye. Montravel is cursed. And tonight we perform for the one that brought the curse upon it. Philip the Good."

He set off up the road again, and Bert could only motion tiredly for the rest of the troupe to follow.

II.

PASCAL APPROACHED THE KING, WHO STOOD STARING OUT THE window of the Keep's northeast tower. "The acrobats you summoned have been spotted approaching from the west, Your Majesty," he said, bowing with one knee bent. He kept his eyes on the cold stone floor as he awaited the king's acknowledgment.

What seemed like minutes passed, and Pascal felt a bead of sweat trickle from his temple, across his cheek, and to the corner of his nose. It tickled and he ached to wipe it away, but he did not. Formality dictated that he maintain his posture of respect until Philip Théophile recognized him.

Despite the ugly clouds roiling outside the open window, the air in the meditation chamber was preternaturally still. The electric tang of charged particles filled Pascal's mouth. The atmosphere within the castle was maintained by magic of a sort that he could not yet comprehend, though his studies brought him closer and closer to enlightenment every day.

More sweat dripped down Pascal's face, and still Philip did not speak. Pascal felt a dangerous tremble beginning in his left leg, the one supporting most of his weight. To shift his position would be a serious breach of protocol, and he fought to keep himself still. He resisted the urge to draw on the Keep's reservoirs of energy to strengthen himself. Now that he thought he knew where that energy came from, he hoped he would never be tempted to draw on it for inconsequential uses again.

But Pascal was not yet as morally incorrupt as he hoped to become. He could not resist opening the third eye he had recently learned to control. The method for conjuring the eye was one of the last bits of lore that Donatien had passed on to Pascal before passing on himself. Insubstantial, the eye floated in the air above his head, unseen but all-seeing. Pascal focused the eye on the king, so still as he leaned on the window sill that he could almost have been a statue clad in gray cotton tights and tunic. Pascal wondered what Philip could possibly be seeing in all that electric fog.

Then the king shifted, leaning his torso out the window, and Pascal felt a nearly irresistible compulsion to rush him, shove him bodily out into the clouds, follow him with the third eye as he fell the thousand-odd feet to his death. Philip certainly deserved such an end, if only for his treatment of young Queen Gabrielle. The only problems were that, first, Pascal did not yet have the evidence he needed of the king's greater crimes, and second, he was not at all certain that even such a great fall would be enough to kill Philip the Good. Pascal had lived at Montravel Keep for ten years, apprenticed to Donatien, and in all that time Philip was the only one of the hundreds of people in the castle who had not seemed to age a single day. Even Donatien, great magician that he was, had been a shrunken and wizened little man when he passed away at the age of sixty—very young for a wizard of his stature.

"Thank you, Pascal," the king said at last, though he still did not turn from the window. "We fear, though, that these are not the acrobats we've been hoping to receive."

Pascal breathed an audible sigh as he straightened up and stretched his cramping leg. "I'm afraid I don't understand, Majesty," he said. "These *are* the acrobats you summoned."

Philip turned suddenly, fixing Pascal with the full force of his ice-blue eyes. Torchlight reflected from those eyes in wraithlike orange pinpricks. His brown beard, which bore the same slight trace of gray that had always graced it, bristled as he compressed his lips. "And how do you know? Have scouts been sent out to meet them?"

Pascal's blood ran cold, as if the chill from the king's eyes had penetrated his veins. "Yes, Majesty," he said, hoping the quaver in his voice would not betray the lie. Philip considered Pascal a foolish and inept pretender who could never equal Donatien's greatness, and Pascal wanted to maintain that appearance. He knew he would be better off without the king suspecting that Pascal could read the lettering on a trunk slung between two men who were still a league away. "They confirm that these men are indeed Jacques Paine and his players."

Philip sighed and turned back to the window. "We'd hoped these were the ones." His regal voice, aimed out the window, seemed to come from a great distance. "They fit the rest of the prophecy. But the clouds are still here. The clouds are still here."

These statements chilled Pascal, though he did not know quite why. "I'm sorry, Majesty," he said. "I don't believe this is a prophecy I'm familiar with."

The king waved a perfunctory hand. "Merely something Donatien mentioned to us once. That thirteen acrobats, traveling on foot, would one day bring with them the cleansing wind that would sweep these damned clouds all away. You realize, Pascal, that there hasn't been a clear day in Montravel for as long as we can remember?" He shook his head, and his shoulders rounded with weariness. "But we suppose we'll just have to keep waiting. We'd wager these fellows weren't even traveling on foot."

The chill Pascal felt intensified, but it no longer filled him with dread. In fact, he felt a glimmer of hope for the first time since Donatien had spotted his talent, plucked him from a hard-scrabble existence in the countryside, and impressed him into service as his apprentice. "No, Majesty," he said, marveling at the fluid way these lies were rolling from his tongue.

"Someday, perhaps. Someday."

Pascal was suddenly very eager to ensure that these acrobats retained their audience with the king. "Shall I have these fellows sent away, Majesty? Seeing as they are not the ones you hoped to receive?"

Philip looked back over his shoulder with a smile that managed to be sad and condescending at the same time. "Ah, how we miss Donatien's wisdom," he said. "Of course you shouldn't send them away. We still need our entertainment, Pascal. These days are dark, and without a bit of merriment to distract us, we might all sink into an irrevocable despair. No, the show will go on, this evening directly after supper."

"Yes, Majesty," Pascal said, bowing to conceal the smile that he could not keep from his lips.

"And be certain that the spell in the theater is strengthened," the king said. "We don't want these acrobats pleading exhaustion in order to cadge an extra night's stay. The show goes on *tonight*."

"Yes, Majesty."

"And be certain that all our court is advised to attend, including our queen. This may not be the troupe we had hoped to receive, but we have been looking forward to their performance from the moment we received their dispatch."

A dispatch? Pascal raised his eyebrows, but did not pursue the questions that filled his mind. He judged that he had probed the limits of the king's patience already during this interview. He would hope for another opportunity to satisfy his curiosity on this point—or attempt to manufacture the opportunity.

"Anything more, Majesty?" Pascal asked.

"No," Philip said. "You are dismissed."

Pascal sketched an elaborate bow. "Thank you, Majesty. I will see that all is in order for tonight's performance."

The king turned back to the window as Pascal backed toward the brassbound door. The torches threw flickering shadows into the corners of the meditation chamber, ghosts that danced at the verges of the room's bare granite walls. It was an austere space. Not even a rug interrupted the cold seams of the floor.

"Pascal," Philip said suddenly.

Pascal was at the door. "Yes, Majesty?" he asked, pausing before he exited.

"We've done our best for Montravel," he said softly, in a voice with an imploring edge, as if he were seeking Pascal's approval. "We've been a good king. Why will these evil days not pass?"

Pity warred with revulsion in Pascal's heart. He did not trust himself to answer this question, so he slipped out the door as quietly as possible. He nodded to the guards standing at attention in the hallway outside, then hurried off in the direction of his own quarters.

He shook his head. Philip the Good really believed that he had been a good king. There should have been a law against a ruler choosing his own soubriquet. It made self-delusion all that much easier. As did the magnum of wine that Philip would consume before evening.

Pascal sighed. He had a great amount of work to do before evening, but first he needed to delve back into Donatien's writings. There was much he still did not understand, and he was curious to know how much of this day the old magician had foreseen.

He was also curious to see if Donatien had left any of his signature cryptic instructions to help Pascal through this critical evening.

III.

BERT MOTIONED FOR THE REST OF THE MEN TO STOP, THEN SET down his end of the heavy chest of costumes. The moment he was free of the load, he felt his head swim and his vision begin to go black. His clothes were pasted to his body with dried sweat and grime. All he wanted to do was to pitch over into the dust and sleep.

But he could not, and neither could any of the rest of the men. They were a scant dozen yards from the Keep. It was time for all the sharpness they could muster.

Jacques did not stop with the others. He continued on toward the high iron portcullis that was the castle's only entrance. The air crackled dryly around them. The malevolent yellow-gray clouds now churned only two or three hundred feet above their heads, and occasional bright flashes from within the clouds outshone the torchlight burning in the passageway beyond the portcullis. Jacques's figure threw a long and wavering shadow as he strode briskly ahead.

Bert heard gratified sighs and the clinking of metal implements from behind him. He turned and saw that fully half the troupe had dropped their loads and sunk to the packed roadbed.

Emile still stood, as did Rene, who tensely followed Jacques's progress with his eyes.

"On your feet, men!" Bert barked, acutely conscious that these men had precious little strength remaining. What energy the long hike uphill had not sapped, the dread presence of the Keep ahead had. "We need to look fresh!"

"My boil-spangled backside," said Guillaume, who had plopped himself down on the other end of the chest and now glared up at Bert from beneath bushy brows. "We'll never be sardin' fresh again, let alone *look* it."

"On your feet!" Bert repeated, standing over Guillaume with his fists on his hips. "This may be the most important performance we'll ever give, and you *will* look fresh, mister, or by God you'll *get* something to complain about. Am I clear?"

Guillaume grumbled something inaudible, but he did push himself back to his feet. The others who were relaxing followed his example.

Bert tried to ignore their wan, drawn faces—he was only doing his job, pushing them so hard—but somehow he could not. He glanced down at his shoes, and thought about how good it would feel to peel them off and soak his feet in hot salted water. "Just last with me through the evening, men," he said softly. "I'll make it up to you, I promise."

Now Bert *really* could not look them in the eyes. Cheeks flushed, he turned to watch Jacques, who had stopped at the portcullis. The stout iron grate was set deep in a granite archway. Human bones had been carved in bas-relief into each stone that made up the arch. Four shadowy forms standing in a loose semicircle beyond the portcullis eclipsed the torchlight streaming from behind them. Bert raised his eyebrows. No guards had been in evidence as the troupe had approached.

Jacques was addressing the guards in a low but forceful tone of voice, though Bert could not make out what he was saying. Bert sensed a presence at his elbow. He turned to see that Emile had drawn up next to him, the sack of cookware still slung over his shoulder. The boy's face shone a sickly yellow in the torchlight. "How are you holding up?" Bert asked him.

Emile's gaze shifted nervously from Jacques and the guards to Bert and then back again. "I'm worried about Beetle and Brow," he said.

"They'll be fine," Bert said. "You turned them loose from the yoke, right?"

Emile nodded.

Bert shrugged. "There you go," he said. "Horses are smart. They'll find food and water somewhere."

"I know," Emile said. His lips drew together tightly, and Bert saw him brush one of his eyes with the back of his hand. The boy stared straight ahead, stolidly.

"We'll find them again," Bert said gently, squeezing the boy's shoulder. "We won't be here long. One performance, then out in the morning. You'll see them again."

"No, I won't."

Bert was shocked by the mature certainty in the boy's voice. He pretended confusion, though Emile's premonition chilled him to the bone. The boy did have a certain measure of magic, after all. "What do you mean, son? They'll know to come back to the wagons once they've found water."

"You know that's not what I mean, Bert." Emile's face seemed to harden in the yellow light as he continued to stare straight ahead. "You've known him for years and years. So tell me—is he really crazy like the other men say?"

Bert felt a hitch in his chest. He knew that some members

of the troupe spoke as if Jacques *were* crazy, but Bert did not like to hear such talk. In fact, he realized with a pang that he loved Jacques—something he had never considered before—and that he was probably hurt by such accusations more than Jacques himself was.

"No, Emile," he said, and the torchlight blurred and softened as his eyes misted, "he's not crazy. He may ask hard things of us, but I've never known him to do it without reason. I think this trek has been the hardest thing he's ever asked of us, so it must be more important than any of us can possibly guess." He wiped his eyes, but did not let his voice crack. "But above everything else, he's fair. He'd never ask anything of us that he wouldn't do first himself. And that's just what he's done today."

Just then, a hideous tortured shriek cut through the heavy air. Bert's heart raced and the steely taste of fear filled his mouth, but after a moment he realized that it was only the great portcullis being raised by a hidden winch. Jacques had taken a few steps back from the opening, and now he motioned for the troupe to join him.

"Showtime," Bert said, glancing over to see how Emile was doing. The boy set his jaw firmly, then strode ahead, lank hair stirring only faintly. Bert heard the men behind him shoulder their burdens. Together with Guillaume, he lifted the heavy costume chest and followed.

Jacques waited at the verge of the open passageway for the others to catch up with him. Rene, his scar an angry white trail, slipped past Bert just before the party reached Jacques. Shoulder to shoulder, Jacques and Rene crossed the threshold into the Keep. Bert felt a twinge of jealousy that the relative newcomer to the troupe should share that position with Jacques, but he swallowed it down. Above all else, Jacques was fair. There was a reason for everything he did, and for everything he allowed.

Emile was next, stumbling a bit as he entered the Keep, then Bert and Guillaume. Just before passing through the arch, Bert glanced up, and he was momentarily horrified to realize that what he had taken for bas-relief carvings of human bones from a distance were actually genuine human bones mortared into the design of the arch.

Then Bert passed into the Keep, flanked by guards clothed in thick leather armor and armed with heavy muskets, and despite the oppressive closeness of the passageway, he felt as if a great weight had suddenly been lifted from his shoulders. Even the chest that he and Guillaume carried between them seemed lighter now. He glanced over at Guillaume, who looked like he didn't know whether to be more relieved or frightened.

The passageway smelled of smoke, tallow, and cool mold, and was wide enough for six men abreast. It was only as they progressed that Bert saw the recessed niches set at angles into each wall, niches which had been completely invisible from outside. Each one concealed another guard, and each guard held a musket at port arms. Bert also spotted the narrow slits in the walls, through with a deadly hail of arrows could be fired. An invading force could easily be pinned down and cut to ribbons in this passageway.

Bert heard the portcullis grind shut behind them, and he glanced back to be sure that all his men were inside. About thirty yards ahead, another iron grate blocked entrance to the castle proper. As they approached, this grate squealed open, revealing a young man of about twenty with dark brown hair. The young man was tall and seemed thin and gaunt, though the deep-blue robes he wore made it impossible to tell for certain. He stood squarely before them with his arms folded, and the escorts halted the party several yards away from him. A cavernous, ill-defined space yawned behind the young man.

"I am Pascal Demain," he said in a reedy, somewhat distracted voice, "court magician and advisor to His Imperial Majesty, Philip the Good. On behalf of the king and queen, who eagerly await your performance, I welcome you to Montravel Keep and bid you good evening."

Bert shivered. Despite the fact that he felt stronger than he had all day, he wanted nothing more than to slip off to sleep in some dark corner of the castle, on a pallet of hay if possible, on the cold stone itself if necessary.

He could sense the approaching darkness as well as Emile could, and he wanted no part in what was coming.

IV.

PASCAL RETRACTED AND CLOSED THE THIRD EYE, BITTERLY DIS-appointed. Even as he mouthed the words of welcome, he had been probing the members of the acting troupe and the bundles they carried for weapons. The newcomers were clean—all but for the lean blond man with the scar, who concealed at least three knives on his person. This man might indeed be an assassin—certainly Pascal took an instant disliking to him—but on the whole, the group left much to be desired as an army of liberation.

If these were indeed the same thirteen acrobats of whom Donatien had prophesied to King Philip, then they probably were not going to accomplish their purpose through a bloody coup.

Then how? How?

The apparent leader of the troupe, a powerful-looking man with long black hair and a black beard, stepped forward and bowed. He held a sack full of weapons, but they were all harmless, carved from wood—props. Pascal could tell that the man was tired, but still his movements were supple and graceful. He bowed low, then raised eyes the color of rich moss. "Jacques Paine at your service, milord," he said, with a genuine humility and submissiveness that took Pascal by surprise. "We're indeed honored by this opportunity to ply our trade before your noble king. Now, may I present my players?"

Jacques Paine straightened and made a motion toward his troupe. The men nodded and bowed. Despite the color returning to their cheeks, Pascal clearly saw their exhaustion and fear. Not what he had been hoping to see. Not at all.

But nonetheless, Pascal tried to match Paine's easy graciousness. "No, it is we who are honored by the presence of such a famed band of actors. It is not every day that we play host to such talent."

Paine nodded gravely. "Thank you, milord. We shall strive not to disappoint you in your expectations."

Pascal felt a strange chill, almost as if Donatien's ghost were hovering at his shoulder. An innocuous enough sentiment, but still . . .

Paine singled out of one his men with a gesture. "Milord, I wish particularly to present my propmaster and right-hand man, Bert Dram. If our performances succeed in any measure at all, then we owe the thanks to Bert, to his hard work and loyalty and discipline behind the scenes. Every endeavor should have its Bert Dram, if it is to be assured of success."

Bert Dram stepped forward, sketching a clumsy but earnest bow. His cheeks were red with more than just restored vigor. He was a man of advancing years, corpulent but strong, with short, wirelike gray hair. "Milord," he murmured.

Pascal nodded at Dram. "It is a singular pleasure," he said, feeling an odd tug of affinity for this man. "My fondest hope is that one day my king may utter words to match those with which your master has praised you today. Such praise is not lightly earned."

Dram muttered something that might have been a thanks, then stepped back, head down, cheeks blazing.

Pascal nodded once more to the troupe as a whole. He thought he detected a hint of jealousy about the countenance of the assassin with the scar. Angry that he hadn't been singled out for praise like Bert Dram? Interesting.

"Again, welcome to Montravel Keep, gentlemen," Pascal said. "Let me show you directly to the theater. I should not like to keep His Imperial Majesty waiting, as I know he eagerly looks forward to your performance."

As do I, Pascal thought. As do I.

V.

The magician turned suddenly on his heel, blue robes swirling, and stalked off through the gloom of the Keep's cavernous great hall. Jacques followed. Bert, cheeks still hot, fought down his embarrassment and barked, "Let's go, men! Hop to it!"

Together Bert and Guillaume hefted the costume chest and set off after Jacques and the magician.

Scattered torches lit the great hall poorly. Bert could see suits of armor lining the distant walls, and far above his head bright banners that seemed at odds with the dark atmosphere of the castle, but he was not concentrating on the physical details that surrounded him. He was still trying to shake off the mortification he felt at the way Jacques had praised him.

Not that Bert had exactly been unhappy with what Jacques had said. Quite the contrary, in fact. It was all very flattering. But Bert liked to stay behind the scenes. He was not used to accepting public acclaim, and he was not accustomed to hearing Jacques deliver it. They had always been two men whose mutual respect was an unspoken but understood given.

Bert scarcely saw the corridors and passageways they passed

through, and he scarcely heard the ringing of the guards' boots as they paced the little troupe. He could not rid his mind of the questions.

Why Jacques's sudden change? Why make Bert into such a public spectacle—especially here and now?

VI.

As Pascal strode through the twisting corridors of the Keep, closer and closer to the theater at its heart, he nearly forgot that he was being followed by thirteen strangers and assorted guards. Scullery maids and ladies-in-waiting, minor functionaries and ministers of state—all stepped aside as the ragged procession wended its way past them, but Pascal registered very little of this. His third eye he had sent ranging through the higher levels of the Keep, in search of the young queen, Gabrielle. His mind was even farther away, still puzzling over what he had learned from Donatien's manuscripts in the short time he had been able to study them before the arrival of the acrobats.

He finally discovered Queen Gabrielle quite by accident. As the eye drifted half-unaware through the twisted corridors and chambers of the Keep's southwest tower, Pascal caught sight of a shivering, pale golden nimbus barely visible between piles of laundry in the collection room. At first he paid no attention to it, but as the eye was about to sail through the wall and into the passageway beyond, something made Pascal wheel the eye about for a final look. The golden nimbus turned out to be the crown of a blonde woman's head, a woman who sat huddled on the floor between heaps of cottons and wools, sables and ermines, knees drawn up to her chest, arms around her knees, and head bowed. Lovely yellow hair spilled over her arms and face, but Pascal had no trouble recognizing the queen.

He could hear no sound through the eye, but it was clear from the way she shook that Gabrielle was weeping.

Pascal allowed the eye to linger on her for a few moments before sending it on to its next destination. He felt a hitch in his chest, and wished that he had a spectral pair of arms he could send upstairs to the collection room to wrap protectively around the young queen, to comfort her against whatever form her grief had taken today. Gabrielle, barely sixteen, was not the sort of woman that Pascal would have chosen for his queen, but she was certainly what he would have ached for if he were marrying for love. How Philip could wed such a lovely girl and then repeatedly abuse her and break her heart . . . it was more than Pascal could fathom.

With a sigh, Pascal sent the eye winging back toward his own chambers. There was nothing he could do to comfort the queen, and even if there had been, it would have been dangerous for him to try. For now, he could only make note of Gabrielle's latest hiding place and be sure that she made it to the theater before curtain time.

As Pascal continued stalking ever nearer to the heart of the Keep, his third eye made its way to the reading table in his inner chamber, where a sheep's-tallow candle still burned in its skull-shaped holder. He trained the eye on the abridgement he had been making of Donatien's manuscripts in the month's since the old magician's death. The work proceeded piecemeal, because often one part of Donatien's writings would make no sense until

Pascal had penetrated a separate, seemingly unrelated section, or until a certain foreseen event had transpired and cast the contents of the manuscripts into a completely new light.

Pascal had for some time now understood that Donatien, during the early years of Philip Théophile's reign, had set up the Keep to act as a sort of magical Lens, gathering and focusing the life energy of Montravel and her people into a force that preserved and sustained the king. Indeed, Donatien used the words "Lens" and "Keep" almost interchangeably in his secret writings. Pascal recognized, even if Philip did not, that it was the king himself who was responsible for the devastation and depopulation of the land. Its stolen life energies were what kept Philip from aging, and what kept his stronghold secure.

Apparently, upon succeeding to the throne, Philip had ordered his confederate Donatien to keep him young and vital and strong, no matter the cost. Donatien had complied. Only in later years had the wizard, himself a victim of the deteriorative effects of the Lens, come to regret the evil he had inflicted on Montravel. He was too far gone in wickedness to be willing to undo the damage himself, but he had chosen Pascal as his apprentice, and had set up a careful progression of knowledge and power that would enable the young magician to do so in his place—though Pascal had not even begun to guess at any of this until after Donatien's death.

One of the most frequently recurring images in Donatien's manuscripts was that of weed and flower. Donatien cast many of his most important concepts in the form of catechetical riddles, which Pascal could not penetrate until he had achieved a certain understanding of their contexts. *Q: Why must we eliminate the weed from the garden? A: Because it steals the strength of the soil away from the flower. Q: But does not the weed have as much claim to the soil as the flower? A: The weed returns no beauty to the world, and it takes far more than simple survival demands . . .*

The implication of passages like this was clear, once Pascal understood the workings of the Lens. The king must be eliminated for the greater good of Montravel. What was not so clear was how and when it was to be done. Donatien's instructions seemed to demand an execution before the king's court—but only after incontrovertible evidence his atrocities had been presented. Pascal had no such evidence, and did not have the faintest idea how to get it. Besides the matter of the Lens, Pascal knew of no outright atrocities Philip had committed, and there were no witnesses remaining from the early days of his reign who could testify against him. Everyone who had been around thirty years earlier when the king ascended to the throne was now dead. They had perished mostly from old age, thanks to the workings of the Lens.

"Damn you, Donatien," Pascal muttered, feeling the full weight of the castle and all its secrets piling up on his shoulders. Donatien had set him what seemed a nearly impossible task, one that the old wizard himself had been too weak to carry out. In fact, Pascal suspected that Donatien had let himself die when he did just so that he would not have to take the responsibility for executing the king himself. "You expect too much from me, you old coward. Far too much."

"I'm sorry, milord. Did you say something?"

The voice was Jacques Paine's, who was keeping pace with Pascal very nearly at his shoulder. Flushing, Pascal snapped back to the here and now, and he momentarily lost contact with the third eye. He had not realized he was speaking out loud. "No, nothing," he said, waving a hand as if to brush away a fly. "I merely let my thoughts carry me away. The theater is just ahead. I hope you'll find it suitable for your program."

"Undoubtedly, milord," Paine said. "Undoubtedly."

Pascal summoned the third eye back and turned it on Paine. The actor looked to be in his mid to late thirties, half again Pascal's age. He moved with self-confidence and grace, despite the long trek he and his troupe had just completed. He was all the things that Pascal was not—handsome, charismatic, regal.

And unassuming. That was perhaps the man's most attractive and compelling characteristic.

Pascal sighed. Paine was the sort of man he would be overjoyed to serve under. Paine's men obviously held a fierce loyalty to him, and it was equally obvious that he treated them well in return. Why else would they follow him across so many leagues of desolate countryside to this forbidding outpost?

Paine and his men had to be the ones Donatien had foreseen. They *had* to be. They would take matters into their own hands, their assassin would execute Philip with his bare hands, and then Pascal would be free of the dread task that an evil old magician had thrust upon him without so much as a by-your-leave . . .

A brightening in the torchlight indicated that they had nearly reached their goal. The corridor here broadened out into a wide, curved passageway, and burning sconces lined both walls at frequent intervals. Three sets of stone stairs led down from the passageway, each entering the theater at a different point on its semicircular circumference. Pascal descended the nearest stairs, Paine and his men close behind. At the bottom of the stairs, an ironbound oak door creaked open at Pascal's touch. He led the way into the pitch-black theater.

Pascal could feel a web of power thrumming all around him. Not only was the theater near the heart of the Keep, it was also the site of the strongest spell in the castle other than the Lens itself. He took a few steps into the dark chamber, then drew an intricate shape in the air with his fingers. A dozen torches flared to life around the outside wall, and a series of braziers fronting the stage gave off a smoky glow.

"I hope the space and lighting here will be satisfactory," Pascal said, turning.

The acrobats huddled together in a knot just inside the door. Only Paine looked unfrightened; his green eyes glowed with appreciative wonder. "This will be more than satisfactory, milord," he said, nodding. "In fact, until now we've only dreamed of performing in such a magnificent space."

Pascal raised his eyebrows and glanced around the theater, trying to view it as if he had never been there before. The ceiling was high and vaulted, acoustically perfect, four times as tall as Pascal himself. Thick columns engraved with comedy and tragedy masks supported the ceiling, while carved stone benches curved in gentle arcs around the deep stage, which was large enough to comfortably fit a troupe of twice as many men as Paine's. The floor sloped downward gently, but enough so that everyone in the audience could have a commanding view of the action. The best seats, however, were the king's and queen's—two solid and massive thrones situated dead-center in the audience. No benches sat fore or aft of the thrones; a wide, unobstructed aisle led directly to them from the front of the stage.

Try as he might, Pascal could see nothing particularly special about the appearance of the theater. It matched the scale and grandeur of the rest of the Keep—which had overwhelmed him ten years ago, but now seemed repetitive and routine. To Pascal, this was simply one more showroom constructed by a madman who valued his entertainment above all else.

But Paine and his players were obviously impressed.

"Go ahead and begin your preparations," Pascal said, gesturing toward the stage. "The king will wish to view your performance as soon as possible."

"Yes, milord." Paine sketched a brief bow, then moved off down the nearest aisle toward the stage, neck craning as he took in all the sights.

"You heard the man," Dram barked roughly to the rest of the players. He stood just inside the door the theater, fists planted immovably on his hips. "Let's move!"

As the laden acrobats spilled into the theater, followed by their armed guards, Pascal glided quietly to the very back of the theater. He had much to do before the performance, and he hoped for another chance to consult Donatien's manuscripts before the show began, but for the moment his next task seemed clear. In an uncharacteristically lucid passage, Donatien had written, *If the king commands you in any matter, it is your sworn duty to obey—particularly when you fear that your obedience may cause injury, loss of life, or other destruction. You must permit these things that the judgments which shall come upon him will be just, and that the blood of the innocent shall stand as a witness against him, and cry out mightily at the last day.*

Or, to paraphrase, you must give him enough rope to hang himself.

Before Pascal was even born, Donatien, at the king's behest, had woven a spell around and through the theater, one which magically strengthened actors and acrobats so they could complete their performances without collapsing from exhaustion. This was particularly important given that merely entering the borders of Montravel depleted men of their energy.

Now Philip had instructed Pascal to strengthen that spell. Pascal feared what would happen as a result of this action—perhaps the players would be unable to stop their performance at all, for any reason—but he set his jaw firmly nonetheless. Donatien's instructions were clear.

He wove his fingers through the invisible strands of the spell, tightening and binding the magical energies as he went along.

Just enough rope for the king to hang himself, he thought all the while. Just enough rope.

VII.

"GATHER 'ROUND, MEN," JACQUES SAID, DUMPING HIS SACK FULL of wooden weapons to the polished floor of the stage. "Let's talk about this evening's program."

Bert barely heard him. Normally he would have been right there at Jacques's side, urging the men to get a move on, but all Bert's attention was on the tall young magician gliding through the shadows at the back of the theater.

"Hey, Bert, let's go," Guillaume said, giving a little tug at the other end of the costume chest.

Bert stumbled in the aisle and nearly lost his balance. "What? Oh, sorry, Guy. I was somewhere else."

"Sardin' 'scrcelled is what you were." Guillaume shook his head and curled his lip in a wry smile, something he rarely did except on stage. "The man in blue weaves his fingers, and you lose all your will power. Like a sardin' puppet with no wires. Hypnotized."

"Shut your gash," Bert snapped, cheeks flushing. Almost immediately he felt guilty for lapsing into low speech—almost as guilty as he felt for snapping at Guillaume in the first place. He normally had more patience with that sort of needling. "I'm not hypnotized."

Guillaume's eyes were wide as he backed down the aisle with his end of the chest. "Sorry, Bert," he said quietly. "Didn't mean nothing by it."

Bert gritted his teeth. He was losing his control, just when Jacques most needed him to keep it together. This place was doing it to him. The Keep. Montravel itself.

And as much as he tried, as he and Guillaume wrested the chest up onto the stage, Bert kept throwing glances back over his shoulder to where the young magician drifted through the shadows at the back of the theater, wiggling his fingers through intricate patterns and mouthing something under his breath.

The magician was up to no good. Bert could sense it.

He and Guillaume let the chest carefully to the surface of the stage, then flopped down on it like a bench, breathing heavily and mopping their brows. They were the last members of the troupe to reach the stage; the others were already gathered around Jacques, expectant.

"Glad you could join us, gentlemen," Jacques said, nodding in Bert's direction. "I trust the march down the aisle was not too great a strain."

Bert lowered his head, sensing the eyes of all the troupe on him and Guillaume. He could not remember the last time he had been singled out for a reprimand. He said nothing in response.

"Look," Jacques said, spreading his arms, "I know everyone is tired, and some of you may even be a little frightened, but there's really nothing here to fear. You're all good men, so you have nothing to fear." He clasped his hands behind his back, pacing before the men, a general reviewing his troops. "We don't have a lot of time, so I'm going to need you all to be sharp, as sharp as you've ever been. The program tonight is not going to be quite what you're used to. The first half—the comedy routines, the magic acts, the music, the acrobatics—will be the same as always. But for the second half, we won't be doing *Everyman* or one of the tragedies or anything like that. We'll be doing *The Usurper*."

Bert's mouth fell open, even as amazed muttering broke out among the troupe. *The Usurper* was a dance-play written by Jacques himself, one they had rehearsed but never performed. It was not even all that good, in Bert's opinion. It had no resolution. Bert had tried to tell Jacques this on many occasions, to suggest rewrites, but Jacques had waved off his objections. "It's not that kind of a story, Bert," Jacques had always said. "You'll understand when we finally perform it."

In no way were they going to pull this performance off. Jacques was going to get them all into a whole kettle of trouble.

Beside Bert, Guillaume was shaking his head and laughing mirthlessly. "One more piece of sardin' craziness to cap off the day," he said, softly so that only Bert could hear.

Bert glanced up at Emile, who was standing nearby—and had turned gray and broken out in a sweat. The poor boy had his biggest role in *The Usurper*. It would be the first time he had filled more than a spear carrier's shoes in any actual performance by the Paine Players . . . but Bert had to wonder how much of Emile's apparent distress was from worry over the performance itself and how much was from the boy's sinister premonitions.

The murmuring went on and on, and Jacques made calming motions with his hands. "All right, all right, let's keep it down," he said, quieting the troupe. "I can see you're worried about this, but there's no reason to be. We're going to do just fine, you'll see.

I wouldn't spring this on you if I didn't have the confidence that you could do what I need you to do. And you will."

He lowered his eyes briefly, then raised them again, bright green and moist. "You're the best there are, men. You're the finest performers I could ever have asked for, and I know you're going to make me proud tonight. Now let's get set up. We couldn't bring all the scenery up from the wagon, so we're going to have to be creative about how we apply it."

This was normally Bert's cue to jump in and start directing the men in their labors. "All right, men," he said listlessly from his perch on the chest, "you heard Jacques. Let's go."

Bert felt the troupe's stares on him again as he stood up, turned his back on them, and began walking up the aisle toward the back of the theater.

"Let's go!" Jacques shouted, clapping his hands, a forced smile in his voice. "Time's short! We all have our jobs to do!"

My lines, Bert thought. Those are my lines.

I'm not needed here. Jacques knows it.

His eyes misted up as he searched the rear of the theater for the magician in blue. He felt an urgent and inexplicable need to speak with the man, even though he was not sure what he intended to say. Plead for all their lives? Beg their way out of this doomed engagement?

It turned out not to matter, though. The guards still lined the walls of the theater, but the magician himself was gone.

"What is he doing to us?" Bert murmured as his tear-blurred eyes turned panned past the guards and back to the stage. A terrible sickness burned in the pit of his stomach. "What?"

Bert was not sure whether he meant Jacques or the magician. He was no longer certain which of them was more dangerous.

VIII.

Weaving a minor spell of comfort, Pascal tried to rid himself of the self-loathing he felt, but it did not seem to work. He still hated himself for what he had just done.

He unlocked his chambers and pushed his way inside, wishing he could wrap himself up in a protective cocoon of darkness and not witness whatever it was that was going to happen shortly in the theater. Donatien's words seemed to absolve Pascal of any responsibility for what could result from the strengthened stage-spell, but Pascal was not so sure the old wizard was right. If the spell worked the way Pascal thought it would, he might just become an accessory to murder.

As he leaned against the inside of the door to close it, Pascal sent his third eye back up to the collection chamber to assure himself that the Queen Gabrielle was still there. She was, though she was no longer sobbing; she had fallen asleep against one of the soft piles of laundry, a delicate fist pressed against her mouth. Pascal focused in on her face for a moment—so beautiful in repose, so peaceful—and then with a heavy sigh of regret, he summoned the eye back to his chambers. He figured he had time for one more consultation with Donatien's manuscripts, and then he would have to see that the queen made it to the theater in time for the night's performance.

The tallow candle still guttered on his reading table in the next chamber, throwing dancing bands of light across the floor beneath the tapestry that covered the inner doorway. Moving the tapestry aside, Pascal entered the chamber. His simple straw pallet occupied one corner of the room, his modest wardrobe another. The rest of the chamber was filled with old books, which lay both open and closed, face up and face down, on every free surface in the room. An oak cabinet filled with pigeonholes covered one entire wall, and rolled scrolls of every age and color poked out from the narrow slots.

Pascal went straight to his reading table, where a scroll of his own—covered with notes in his cramped, spidery hand—was held open by two lead weights. He removed the weights and let the scroll roll itself shut, then went to the cabinet and hunted for the manuscript he wanted. After a few moments of searching, he drew from the upper-right quadrant of the cabinet a parchment scroll that had begun to yellow but was otherwise still supple. Unrolling the scroll on the reading table, Pascal opened his third eye and trained it on Donatien's solid, blocky handwriting.

This was one more useful application for the eye. Donatien's manuscripts were all encrypted, and only by viewing them through the third eye could Pascal make out the old magician's true words. Understanding them, however, was an entirely different matter.

Pascal thought he remembered a reference to "the Time of the Thirteen" from this particular scroll. He had once thought that Donatien might have been referring in some way to a specific time of the day, an hour of the clock, but now Pascal realized that it was probably a allusion to the arrival of the thirteen acrobats. He scanned the parchment sheet rapidly, and near the bottom of the page he found what he was seeking:

. . . and in the Time of the Thirteen, you will see that all things turn, and that both the just and the unjust receive their due. The large shall be made small, and the small shall be made large, even as a viewing-scope, when turned, can be made to reverse the image it projects . . .

"Great Maker," Pascal breathed, sitting back on his stool, eyes wide. He read the passage through again, then stared unseeing through the far wall of the chamber, his mind a blur.

What was a viewing-scope but a tube with lenses mounted inside. Lenses! Why had he not seen this before?

Pascal read the passage through one more time, then kept going to the bottom of the page. There were the instructions he needed, now that he finally understood the need—instructions as to how a man could be installed at the focus of the Lens, and how its destructive powers could be reversed, and the lushness of the countryside restored.

The only question now remaining was how to lure Philip to the focus of the Lens, and then keep him there.

Pascal stood up from the reading table, so suddenly that his stool clattered over backward. His heart pounded with excitement. Tonight he would save the kingdom of Montravel. Tonight!

He sent the eye flashing down through level after level of the Keep, until it emerged into the smoky light of the theater. The players were hammering together the last of their scant scenery, and it seemed that their rehearsals were almost over.

Nearly time for the show.

Pascal summoned the eye back, settling his robes about his

shoulders and setting off for the southwest collection chamber, where Gabrielle still slept serenely. As the eye approached, he glanced through it for a moment, unthinking, and was briefly startled to see himself as he exited from his personal chambers. He watched himself stiffen in surprise, for he had never before thought to use the eye to view himself from the outside.

He was dismayed to see a few silver hairs woven in with the brown at his temples, and to see the fine wrinkles that were forming at the corners of his eyes.

Pascal was not yet twenty-four years old.

He hurried off down the passageway, sending the eye far ahead to scout the way—far ahead, where he would be unable to catch another unintended glimpse of his first signs of aging.

But hurry as he would, Pascal could still not outrace the chill that pursued him.

IX.

BERT HAD WAITED AND WAITED IN THE SHADOWS AT THE BACK of the theater for Jacques to come to him, to reprimand him for turning his back on the troupe, to order him back to the stage where the assembly of the scenery was nearly complete. But it did not happen, and finally Bert grew weary of the self-pitying pose he had assumed. He picked his way silently, unobtrusively, down the far aisle of the theater, then climbed up onto the edge of the stage.

Guillaume Roe nodded gravely to Bert from center stage, where he and Claude Villy were putting the finishing touches on a flimsy, makeshift throne they had assembled from building materials scattered about backstage. Guillaume seemed to be welcoming Bert back to the fold, but it was Emile who broke away from the crew of actors turned craftsmen and joined Bert where he stood wringing his hands.

"Are you all right, Bert?" Emile asked. "When you walked away from everyone, I . . . well, I didn't know what to think."

Bert noted the boy's pale cheeks, his hollow eyes. "Sorry," he said quietly, not meeting Emile's gaze. "I guess the pressure was just getting to me. Not a good time to break down."

The other players were watching Bert and Emile surreptitiously as they worked, and Bert was very conscious of their glances. He began to turn away from Emile, but the boy stopped him with a hand to his shoulder.

"Bert," Emile said, his voice low and measured, "you feel it too, don't you."

Bert chewed on the inside of his lower lip, let his gaze wander around the stage, and finally looked Emile in the eyes. He could not lie to the boy any longer. "Yes, I do."

Emile nodded gravely and bowed his head. "And do you still think Jacques is right to ask us to do this?"

"Are you worried about the part? If you are, then—"

"I don't care about the part," Emile said. "Not that much, anyway. I'm worried about *all* of us. I just want to know how *you* feel about all this."

Bert raised his eyebrows. "I don't know," he said. "I honestly don't know right now. I plan to talk to him about that."

"He and Rene wandered off backstage together a few minutes ago," Emile said, pointing to a archway in the wings. "I think they were arguing." The boy pressed his lips together and then took a deep breath. "You know, Bert, for what it's worth, I still think Jacques has a good reason for doing this—whatever it is he's doing. I've been trying to look at it from the perspective you gave me back at the castle gate."

Bert shook his head. "I don't know what I'm talking about half the time. Let me just have a word with Jacques. Excuse me." He turned toward the backstage arch without another glance at Emile.

His heart pounded as he moved into the dim shadows backstage. Ropes hung everywhere, strung from pulleys lost far in the darkness overhead, brushing against him like strands from a gigantic spider's web. Forceful whispers came from somewhere up ahead, disembodied voices that gave Bert a chill. Squinting, he passed a rickety wooden ladder, then saw the cape of Rene's elaborate costume sticking out from behind a support column as wide as two men.

Bert drew closer, moving as silently as he could on the cold stone floor.

". . . have to follow the script?" Rene was saying, his voice breathy and wroth. Bert heard the slinky metallic hiss of a knife being drawn, and he stiffened. "Just let us dance up the aisle, and I can have this out and slit the old bastard's throat before anyone knows what happened."

"That's just it," Jacques said, concealed behind the column. Bert let his breath out in a relieved sigh. For a moment he had thought that Rene meant to kill Jacques. "We want *everyone* to know what happens when it happens. There can't be any doubt in anyone's mind that what happens is just. If we're lucky, we may not even have to kill him ourselves."

Bert drew a surprised breath as he realized that Jacques and Rene were talking about regicide. He crept closer to the column, trying to stay out of sight.

"That's the whole reason I signed on with you, Jacques!" Rene said, his voice rising in pitch. "You promised I'd get the chance to kill him."

"I said you'd get the chance to *be* there. And you still may get the chance, depending on what happens."

"But—"

"No but's, Rene! You'll do it my way, or you won't participate at all!"

"Your way will probably get us killed, Jacques!"

"Your way will *definitely* get us killed—all of us!"

"Yes, but at least we'll go out with glory, and we'll be sure we take him with us!"

Jacques's voice sank to a raw whisper. "Rene, if you don't promise me right now to do as you've been instructed, then I swear to God I'll kill you where you stand."

Bert shivered and flattened himself against the column. He had never heard such menace in Jacques's voice. He wanted to see what was happening, but did not dare move.

A shrill stillness followed. "You couldn't," Rene said after a moment, but his voice was less self-assured than before.

"Try me," Jacques said. Bert heard leather creak and pictured Jacques assuming a fighter's stance. "I'll do it with my bare hands. Promise me *now*."

After another short but tense silence, Bert heard Rene hiss, "Fine. I promise."

Then Rene strode stiffly around the column, a dagger still ready in his hand.

He stopped, eyes widening, when he caught sight of Bert.

"What did you hear?" Rene said in a snarl, raising the dagger and taking a step toward Bert. His eyes narrowed, and the puckered scar across his face turned white.

Bert pressed himself flat against the column, trembling. "Nothing. Nothing at all."

"I doubt that very much," Rene said, clamping a hand on Bert's shoulder and weaving the dagger back and forth a few inches from Bert's face, very much as he did during performances.

Bert felt hypnotized by the moving tip of the blade.

"Put that away!" Jacques said, coming around the column from the other direction. Bert wanted to look at him for comfort, but could not take his eyes away from the blade. "He's one of us, for the love of all that's holy."

"There *are* no others of us," Rene said, but he released Bert and put the dagger away nevertheless. His eyes did not, however, leave Bert's face.

"What are you talking about, Jacques?" Bert said, his voice unsteady. He glanced rapidly back and forth between Jacques and Rene, moving away from the column so he would have somewhere to run if necessary.

Jacques's face with stiff with anger, and he did not look away from Rene. "It's all right, Bert. You don't have to pretend anymore. Leave us, Rene. *Now.*"

Rene glared at Jacques for a moment, then spun on his heel and strode back to the stage.

Bert rubbed his shoulder, wincing, where Rene's fingers had dug in. "What was *that* all about?"

"It depends," Jacques said. "How much did you hear?"

"Enough."

Jacques locked at the floor for a few moments, lips pursed. In the backstage shadows, his prominent cheekbones turned his face to a bearded skull. "I've been meaning to talk to you all evening," he said. "I don't blame you for not liking this situation, Bert. I know I haven't confided in you on this at all, but I need to ask you to trust me for a little while longer."

Bert felt a constrictive emotion rising in his throat, and he realized it was jealousy that Jacques had confided more in Rene than in him. "Look me in the eyes and ask me," he said, feeling the corners of his mouth twitch.

Jacques raised his head and looked Bert squarely in the face. His green eyes glowed with mute appeal in the dimness. "Please, Bert," he said. "Trust me for a little while longer. I've never led you astray yet, and I need you now."

Bert's eyes moistened. "I don't understand, Jacques. You need me for what?"

Jacques reached inside the laces of his shirt, where a leather pouch hung from a thong around his neck. He pulled open the pouch and shook a small object out into his hand. "Do you have a pocket?"

Bert touched the side of his trousers. "Yes, of course."

Jacques crossed the distance between them, holding the small object up to his face. He wore an expression of longing. "Keep this for me, Bert," he said, and after a moment's hesitation he put the object into Bert's hand. "And if anything happens to me this evening, I want you to take my place."

Bert peered at the object in his hand. It was a silver signet ring. A jagged mountaintop had been carved into the face of the ring, inset in a field of bright rubies. "I can't," Bert said, shaking his head and holding the ring out to Jacques. "I can't take this."

Jacques held up his hand, palm out. "I want you to. Please."

Bert examined the ring again. "But why?"

"I've wanted this from the beginning," Jacques said, looking off into the shadows. "That's why I picked you so many years ago." He looked back at Bert. "If anything happens to me, take my place."

"But—"

"Please."

Bert shook his head in resignation, then slipped the ring into his trousers pocket. "All right."

"Good," Jacques said, and he suddenly looked as if a great weight had been taken off his shoulders. "Thank you."

Then he, too, turned on his heel and walked back out to the stage.

Bert remained in the shadows backstage for several minutes,

realizing how empty he felt at the prospect of leading the Paine Players in place of Jacques Paine himself, and realizing how little he really knew about Jacques to begin with.

I can't take your place, Jacques, he thought. No one can.

But Bert had made a promise. He only hoped he would not actually have to act on it.

X.

PASCAL ENTERED THE COLLECTION CHAMBER. THE DOOR HAD been bolted from the inside when he arrived, but he knew a spell to unlock the simple mechanism at a touch.

"Your Highness?" he called softly, treading between the piles of soiled laundry. Garments from the entire southwest quadrant of the Keep were brought here for sorting before the charwomen transported them to the lower levels for cleaning, though the work seemed to have fallen behind of late. The smells of mildew and stale sweat filled the air. "Wake up, please, Your Highness. The king requests your immediate presence at a special acrobatic performance in the theater."

Pascal heard a rustle from the darker reaches of the chamber. He walked unerringly to the spot where Gabrielle was trying to burrow her way beneath a high pile of linen. He had sent the eye scouting ahead before he even reached the collection chamber, and he knew the queen was still here, trying to hide.

"Go away, Pascal," she said, her voice muffled. Only the hem of her skirts protruded from beneath the stack. "You never saw me. You don't know I'm here."

Pascal squatted near Gabrielle's feet. He rubbed the stubble on the lower half of his face with one hand, his heart swelling. "I'm sorry, Highness, but I can't do that. My orders are directly from the king. And we both know you'll only make things harder on yourself if you keep this up. Respectfully."

A few moments of silence followed, and Pascal had to fight not to reach out and caress the queen's foot. She was far beyond his reach, if not by virtue of her marriage then certainly from the standpoint of social position. Then he heard the sobbing begin again, and he could not help himself. He touched her ankle, lightly, but an electric thrill still ran up his arm.

"Please, Highness," he said. "I follow the king's orders not to be cruel, but because I must. Believe me when I say I share your grief at your situation, but we must both do our duties. That's what it means to be queen."

Gabrielle crawled out from beneath the pile of laundry then, her golden hair in disarray, her face blotchy and streaked with tears. Wrinkled creased her white satin gown, and the imprints of irregular seams and folds marked her cheeks and neck. She sniffled, and Pascal extended a hand and helped her to her feet.

He had never known anyone more beautiful.

"I'm sorry to be such a trial to you, Pascal," she said, wiping the sleeve of her gown across her face. "I know what I have to do. It's just that—that—"

Then her face crumpled, and tears spilled down her cheeks again.

Pascal drew a silk handkerchief from out of his robes, then dabbed with it at the queen's tears. He towered over her by at least eight inches. She turned her face up to him, her full, sensuous lips and strong jaw contrasting sharply with the childlike appeal of her gray eyes. And she *is* still a child, Pascal reminded himself. And she is the queen.

She waited patiently while he wiped the tears from her cheeks. When he was finished and had thrown the handkerchief onto the nearest pile of laundry, she said, "Thank you, Pascal. You are too good for me. Too good for your own good, I fear." Then she slipped her arms around his waist and embraced him, her hands flat against his back.

Pascal could not breathe. All he could feel was the warmth of her slender body, the pleasant pressure of her head as she rested her cheek against the center of his chest. His hands fluttered helplessly, and he wondered what to do with them. He had never been touched like this by a woman.

He finally rested one hand gingerly on her back, and with the other he stroked her fine, straight hair. A curious queasiness filled his stomach, and he began to tremble. He was very conscious of the unlocked door, and he wished he could bolt it shut from a distance.

His eyes drifted shut for a moment. He had dreamed of a moment like this from the first time he saw Gabrielle—from the moment the king had brought her back from the countryside to be his third queen. She had been filled with wonder and awe as she was first installed in the castle, but Pascal had known what was to come. Neither of the two previous queens had borne Philip any children, and they had both aged rapidly. Pascal was not certain whether they had actually died of natural causes, or whether the king had murdered them.

All he knew was that he would not allow the same thing to happen to the beautiful, delicate girl in his arms. She had not yet missed her blooding, despite the violent and fervid way Philip tried to impregnate her—which Pascal had witnessed once, on a weak occasion, through the third eye. The king would never admit that the fault for it might be his own, and Gabrielle would be the one who suffered.

She had not yet been queen for a year. Pascal vowed that she would live to the end of her natural years. A full lifespan.

He opened his eyes, let his hand fall from her hair, gripped her firmly by the shoulders. "Highness," he said, hunching to look her directly in the eyes, "we must go. And this must not happen again."

Gabrielle touched his cheek, nodding. "I know," she said. Then she cupped her entire hand against his face. "Why are you so good to me, Pascal?"

Because I love you, he thought, and a warm shiver climbed his spine.

"Because you deserve it, Gabrielle," he said. "Your Highness, I mean. Now let me escort you downstairs to the theater. The king is waiting."

Queen Gabrielle squared her shoulders, straightened her gown, ran her fingers through her hair. Then she nodded. "Lead the way, Pascal."

As he held open the door for her and she passed close by him, Pascal clenched his jaw firmly. He ached to touch her again, but that would not be possible.

It would probably never be possible.

XI.

THE TORCHES HAD BEEN DOUSED, AND NOW THE ONLY LIGHT IN the theater was the orange glow from the braziers spaced along the front of the stage. Bert peered out at the audience from the wings, Rene fidgeting anxiously at his shoulder.

"Do you mind?" Bert whispered, glaring back at Rene.

"I only want to see him," Rene said.

"You'll get your chance. He's right there dead-center in the audience. He's the one in the big throne. You can't miss him. Now step back and give me some room to breathe."

Rene's eyes narrowed, but he took a few steps back to where the rest of the troupe waited inside the backstage archway. Jacques stood apart from the others, head bowed, hands clasped behind his back, lips moving soundlessly. Emile stared at the ceiling. Guillaume and Claude and Xavier and Luc and Maurice and all the rest stood together, silently sharing their support.

I couldn't possibly hold these men together without Jacques, Bert thought. The show must go perfectly. It must.

If only he understood Jacques's purpose, his plan.

Bert stared out into the audience at King Philip the Good,

the man who was apparently marked for death that night. He was a striking man—well-built, handsome, regal, crowned with a circlet of gold, and wearing a ceremonial dagger and pistol beneath his sable cloak—but he shifted in the oversized throne like an impatient child, tapping his fingers on the armrest, repeatedly twisting himself around to stare at the entrances, pounding on the seat of the empty throne beside him, slumping down in his own seat in aggrieved fits of pique. The courtiers who filled the benches behaved themselves with much more decorum in Bert's opinion, awaiting the arrival that would signal the start of the performance.

In fact, if Bert were to venture a guess, he might have said that the king was a little drunk.

Then a ray of light spilled into the darkened theater, and the tall magician in blue escorted an exquisite young woman into the theater and to her throne. Everyone but the king rose from their seats, and Bert's breath caught in his throat. The queen was no more than a girl, but he had never seen a girl so beautiful. She held herself proudly, but Bert could tell from the set of her jaw that she was not happy. He let out a sorrowful breath.

The magician waited until the queen was seated, then strode to the front of the stage. The courtiers seated themselves. King Philip leaned over to his young queen, seized her wrist, and whispered something to her fiercely. Bert saw the girl flinch, but she did not lose her pose of nobility.

She wears the rank far better than he does, Bert thought. He doesn't deserve her.

The magician faced the audience, raised his chin. "Your Imperial Majesty," he said, bowing to the king. "Your Royal Highness. Assembled nobles, courtiers, and gentlefolk. By high command of the king himself I present to you, in a program of daring acrobatics, music, low comedy, and high drama, the world-renowned Jacques Paine and the Paine Players!"

With a flourish, the magician gestured toward the archway where the players awaited.

"Let's go!" Bert hissed to the troupe, even as Jacques strode majestically past him and out onto the stage.

The theater resounded with applause and shouts of approval as Jacques pirouetted, spread his arms, and bowed.

The rest of the troupe filed past Bert and into the smoky light of the stage. "Break a leg, men," Bert whispered.

Rene was passing by Bert at the lag end of the file. "We'll break more than that, believe me," he said, patting one of his concealed knives and nodding gravely, as if Bert were now a trusted member of the inner circle.

I don't know *what* I am, Bert thought, folding his arms across his chest. The props were all set up backstage, and there was nothing more for him to do during this first half-hour of the program but watch.

He only wished he had some warm milk to settle his stomach.

XII.

"This is really something," the king said, leaning far to his left over the armrest of the throne, and not bothering to keep his voice down. "Have you ever seen the likes of it, Pascal?"

"No, Majesty," Pascal said. "Never."

"It even beats an evening in the royal bedchambers, hey?"

"I wouldn't know, Majesty." Pascal stared straight ahead at the stage, flushing furiously. "That opportunity has never been my pleasure."

The king roared with laughter, and the courtiers nearby tried not to pay any attention. "We'll have to have ourselves a little fête there sometime, hey? You, we, and a couple of my favorite charwomen."

Pascal tried to ignore the Philip, tried to swallow down his simmering rage. Despite the uneasy tension that continued to build in him, he had to admit that he was as impressed by the show as the king was. The Paine Players proved themselves time and again to be consummate performers, and Jacques Paine himself was as skilled and eloquent a master of ceremonies as Pascal had ever seen. Paine introduced act after act with a grandiosity that seemed impossible for the the performers to live up to, but somehow they did, every time—often actually exceeding the expectations that Paine had created in the audience. A wide variety of entertainments succeeded across the stage—juggling acts, comedy routines, mime performances, musical numbers accompanied by lute and fife, acrobatic spectacles, stunts with fire and knives, conjuring tricks which amazed even Pascal—and on occasion Paine himself would participate in the action, much to the delight of the less inhibited ladies-in-waiting. All in all, it was a fine program, far superior to the offerings of most of the straggling bands of performers who made their way to Montravel Keep.

But Pascal could not enjoy the program nearly as much as he wished to. For one, the performers were beginning to look tired by the end of the first half-hour, and by the end of the hour they were looking positively fatigued. Still, the action never flagged, and while Pascal knew that some of the reason for that was the seasoned professionalism of the troupe, he also knew that it was attributable in great part to Donatien's stage-spell. Pascal never enjoyed seeing performers struggling along at the edge of exhaustion under the influence of magic, but the fine way these men were bearing up under the night's strain pierced him to the heart.

Pascal still did not know what effect the strengthening of the spell would ultimately have on these players. He wanted to enjoy the show wholeheartedly, but when that enjoyment might come at the cost of harm or injury, he simply could not lose himself completely in the spectacle.

And for another thing, he could not stop glancing over at the queen, to see how she was enjoying the show. Pascal was seated directly to Philip's left, at the end of a crowded bench, while

Gabrielle was seated in the throne to the king's right. Philip shouted, guffawed, and catcalled more loudly than anyone else in the crowd, clapping his hands and shifting about in his seat like a drunken child of five. Gabrielle remained more still, but she too clapped and smiled at times. Her smiles warmed Pascal's heart, but inevitably her gaze would steal to the left, toward her husband, and all trace of happiness would vanish from her face.

A particularly ribald comedy routine about a eunuch in a brothel was just coming to a close, one which placed several of the players on stage dressed as harlots, and King Philip leaned across the gap that separated his throne from the rest of the audience to poke Pascal in the shoulder, as he had done a dozen times already that evening. "Now *that's* what we call prime talent," he said with a coarse wink, the sour smell of alcohol wafting from his mouth. A thin line of spit trailed from the corner of the king's mouth. "We almost wouldn't mind getting a piece of that ourselves!"

Pascal shuddered at the lascivious look in the king's blue eyes. "They certainly are adept performers, Your Majesty," he said evenly.

"Probably better than anything we can get here," Philip said. "The Keep's a little short on good talent—if you follow what we mean—and those boys really know how to *act!*"

Fighting to keep the revulsion from his face, Pascal glanced past Philip to Gabrielle. She sat very still, very erect, but the corner of her mouth trembled ever so slightly.

She had heard the king's comment.

"I'm certain they can give you exactly what you need, Your Majesty," Pascal said, turning away from Philip. It was all he could do to keep himself in his seat, not to cross to the queen's throne and take her in his arms and spirit her away into the night.

I want to be watching when they kill you, Philip the Good, he thought. I want to spit in your face and tell you what a worthless wretch you are. I want to hold up a mirror to your soul and watch you cringe in horror at what you've become. Queen Gabrielle deserves so much more than you. Montravel itself deserves so much more than you.

From that moment forward, despite all the action on stage, the greatest suspense of the evening for Pascal was looking forward to finding out whether or not this would be the night that Philip at last met his judgment.

For Pascal had an experiment with the Lens that he was absolutely dying to try out, and that was one show in which Philip the Good would be the star.

XIII.

"I WANT YOU TO BE READY, BERT," JACQUES SAID IN A LOW VOICE as he rapidly changed his costume in the wings. "Things may start happening, and if they do I want you to stay right out of it. You're not to draw any attention to yourself, and you're to save yourself before any of the rest of us. Do I make myself clear?"

As Jacques settled the purple crushed velvet cape around his shoulders, Bert handed him a flowing gray wig. "Oh, yes, very clear," Bert said, glancing around at the others as they milled about readying themselves for the pièce de résistance of the night's performance. "But I don't mind telling you, Jacques, I don't like the idea one bit. Not a bit."

Jacques bent forward so that his long black hair fell forward over his face, then slipped the wig into place. As he straightened, he tossed his hair back he smoothed the gray locks into place. "Your instructions are not to like it," he said, breathing a bit heavily. Sweat ran down his face, and his eyes were hollow and dark. "Your instructions are to do what I say." Jacques held up a hand-mirror, examined himself. "More powder, Bert."

Bert shook his head as he patted powder onto Jacques's face

with a fuzzy cloth buff. Jacques looked like he was about to drop, but Bert knew better than to tell him to slow down. "I never said I wouldn't do it. I just have to tell you that I don't understand what makes me any more important than anyone else."

One corner of Jacques's mouth turned up in a tired smile. "You *are* no more important than any of the rest of us. It's just that we each have our own rôle to play. Ours is to perform this play and not stop for any reason until it's done, and yours is to stay safe. Just in case."

"Yeah." Bert set the buff down on a rickety wooden table, then picked up a chalky gray stick. He carefully applied the gray to selected sections of Jacques's beard. "Just in case you go and get your bloody throat cut. And for what? For the life of a king in some country no one's ever even heard of?"

Jacques closed his eyes for a moment, looking as if he might slip off into sleep. "You'll understand, Bert," he said, nodding gently. "You'll understand."

On stage, Claude was just bowing at the close of a particularly involved but not very difficult escape illusion. The audience roared its approval, but the voice of King Philip could be heard above all the rest: "Bravo! Come back and teach that one to our queen! She'd love you forever! Hah!"

Jacques's eyes sprang open, a look of distaste spasming across his face. "It's time," he said. Then he squared his shoulders, tossed the cape back over one shoulder, and became a king in one brief moment.

Claude motioned Emile, who had been his assistant for the illusion, out onto stage from the wings. The two of them bowed together, then walked off stage. Matthieu and Jean-David hurried out to retrieve the props from the stage and set new ones in place.

Jacques stood like a statue inside the archway.

Bert seized Emile by the arm and he and Claude walked past. "Are you all right, boy?"

Emile wiped his sweating brow. His skin was sallow and clammy. "Just a little . . . a little tired is all," he said, shaking droplets from his hair.

"Come over here, come over here," Bert said, taking Emile by the arm and guiding him toward a chair. "You've got to have some rest."

Emile followed docilely for a moment, then suddenly stiffened. He planted his feet, and Bert could not move him. "I can't," he said, shaking his head listlessly. "I have to . . . have to change for the next bit."

"Not on your life," Bert said, his jaw clenching. "Jacques can use all the rest of us and that's just fine, but you're just—just a boy. You're not going on. Auguste is young. He can take your place."

Bert tugged on Emile's arm again, but in an impossible show of strength and agility the boy yanked himself out of Bert's grasp and danced a few steps back. He moved jerkily, almost like a marionette. "Auguste plays the advisor to the usurper," he said. "There's no one to replace *him*."

"Then I'll do it myself, by damn!" Bert took a step toward Emile, but the boy danced even further away, dodging between Guillaume and Maurice, who were freshening their makeup.

"You're too old," Emile said, skipping away.

"Hey, what's the sardin' trouble here?" Guillaume said. "We've got a show here, Bert."

Bert slumped, despair washing over him. Were there no choice for any of them?

"I know, Guy," he said. "I know."

He somehow found his way back to the chair in which he had wanted Emile to rest, and as he sank down into it, eyes brimming, he watched a wavery image of Jacques stride out onto the stage.

"Curtain," Bert murmured.

XIV.

When Jacques Paine motioned for quiet, even the king himself fell silent. The stage was bare but for him and a wooden mockup of a throne, pushed off to the left.

Pascal felt his heart beating faster. Paine was dressed in a close-fitting royal-purple doublet, a high collar, silken pantaloons, and a velvet cape trimmed with white fur. His hair was now long and gray, and silver streaks ran through his beard. He looked every inch a king.

This was the moment Pascal had been waiting for. He could sense it.

"Royals, nobles, gathered gentlefolk," Paine said, his clear voice ringing through the theater like a bell, "for the final segment of our performance this evening, the Paine Players are proud to present the world-premier performance of a short play written specifically in honor of His Imperial Majesty, King Philip Théophile of Montravel."

"Hear, hear!" Philip cried, standing up and sketching a wobbly bow toward the stage. The audience clapped, and Queen Gabrielle took advantage of the moment to gaze directly at Pascal.

Save me from this monster, she mouthed with her exquisite lips.

Pascal felt his stomach clench, even as a warm shiver radiated from the center of his chest. Her gray eyes were so clear and compelling that he could only incline his head in a slight nod before returning his gaze to the stage.

Paine returned the king's bow, and Philip sat heavily back in his throne. "I thank you, Your Majesty," Paine said, "and it is my sincerest wish that our humble play will bring you all the joy we felt in preparing it. We shall present this drama in a style borrowed from the mysterious Kibbuko of the lee shores of the eastern continent, who perform their tales all in dance. A narrator will clarify the action. And now it is my extreme pleasure to present the Paine Players in . . . *The Usurper.*"

As the audience applauded, Paine spun, his cape floating on the wind of his passage, and settled himself into the mock throne. Three musicians moved onto the stage, armed with lute, fife, and drum, and began playing a tranquil melody.

A thickset man with curly graying hair appeared at the front corner of the stage, a few sheets of parchment clutched in his hand. "I am Guillaume Roe, your narrator," the man said, his voice more tentative than Paine's. "Welcome to our tale."

Roe shuffled his papers, donned a pair of small, round spectacles, then began to read. "The story takes place in a small kingdom, far, far away, a kingdom so inconsequential that few people had heard of it, and even fewer cared to visit. But to the inhabitants of the land, it was the most beautiful place on earth, and they rejoiced day and night to live out their days in a setting of such undisturbed splendor."

The music stepped up a notch in pace, and several men, some dressed as peasant women, entered the scene, dancing and capering as if they had no cares in the world.

Pascal felt a strange longing deep in his heart. Oh, to have grown up in such a land! To have live and marry and die in peace, perhaps with Gabrielle at his side . . .

"Ah, someone has at last thought to write of Montravel," Philip said loudly to Pascal, poking him again in the shoulder and laughing. "This should make for a fine entertainment."

Pascal looked sidelong at the king, wondering from where a comment like that had come.

On stage, Paine nodded his head and tapped his feet in time with the music, with the steps of the dancing villagers. "And why were the people able to live in such joy?" Roe continued. "For they were ruled by a wise and good king, one who did not hesitate to work beside his people in their fields, who did not burden them with sore taxes, and whose only aim was harmony and trust among all who entered the borders of his land."

Then Paine rose from his throne and joined the villagers in their dance. Pascal was interested to see that Paine did not dominate the dance, though he was obviously the most skilled performer. Rather, his steps were designed to blend harmoniously with the whole, and to make his companions look all the better.

"Ah, yes!" Philip exclaimed. "A true king indeed!"

Pascal shook his head. An appreciation of irony was not one of Philip's strong points.

After a few moments, a young boy in a dress and a long black wig entered the dance, and before long Paine and the boy were dancing together. "The king had lived alone for many years, content merely to labor with his people, when at last a love of a different sort struck him to the heart."

"We'll say!" Philip cried. "A different sort! That's for certain!" A few members of the audience laughed along with him.

Pascal glanced over at Gabrielle, who looked as if she wanted to melt right into her throne.

"She was a young village girl who had only just blossomed into womanhood. The king immediately asked for her hand, and the entire land rejoiced as she became his queen."

Again the tenor of the music changed, and the happy dancing turned into a wedding processional that led right off the stage.

Roe adjusted his spectacles as the processional vanished through the archway behind him. "Before long, a son and heir was born to the newlyweds, and all the land gave thanks that the royal line would not die out."

Paine and the boy-as-queen had returned to the stage, and the boy seated himself in the throne, a doll cradled gently in his arms, as Paine looked over them both with open adoration.

Pascal realized that the king had fallen uncharacteristically silent. Perhaps this struck a little close to home. Good.

As if to underscore his thoughts, the music took a subtle but sinister slide into a minor key.

"But all was not well in the small land, despite the love between the king and the queen and the prince and their people. For a jealous and lazy advisor, angry that the people and especially the queen did not seem to love him as they loved the king, was plotting the overthrow of the kingdom."

From the far side of the stage, a bearded man dressed all in black slinked onto the stage, bowing to the king, kissing the queen's hand, but doing it all with an slippery unctuousness that put Pascal in mind of a snake.

"The advisor had for so long allowed hate and jealousy to canker his heart that he could no longer feel true love, and he believed that the only way he could ever be happy was to destroy the king utterly, and lay waste to his land."

The man in black danced reservedly around the stage, every now and then bending to speak words of flattery into the ears of the king and queen.

"Some perhaps would fault the king for retaining such a man as his closest advisor, but the king was so good-hearted that he could not believe any other man capable of evil. And so when the advisor informed the king that an important matter required his immediate and solitary attention, the king let himself be led to his inner chambers—where tragedy awaited."

Paine followed the man in black across the stage, his purposeful stride a brilliant counterpoint to the advisor's oozing glide.

As they drew to a halt at the far edge of the stage, the man in black drew a club from inside his clothing, whirled with dervish glee, and struck Paine a mighty blow across the back of the head. Paine toppled to the floor. The narrator fell silent and the music built to a frenzy as the advisor broke into a capering, cavorting dance, accompanied by boos and hisses from the audience.

Pascal glanced over at Philip. The king was fidgeting more than usual, shifting back and forth in his seat and tapping his foot on the floor.

During the dance, a man in the costume of a wet nurse, carrying a doll of his own, had approached the queen and taken the baby from her arms for a feeding, then retired from the stage. Thus, the queen was alone when the advisor suddenly crossed the stage, now brandishing a knife, and stabbed the queen through the chest. False blood poured across the bodice of the boy's costume, and the man in black caught the body as it fell.

Philip's foot tapped even faster, and he twitched several times as if he might stand up.

The fife shrieked like a banshee as the advisor, in a stylized routine, ravished the queen's body. When he stood at last, her heart lay in his hand, and many audience members groaned in revulsion.

"The foulest of deeds done," Roe narrated, "all that remained was for the advisor to lay the blame for the crime squarely on the man he hated more than any other. He—"

The man in black, heart in hand, had crossed halfway to Paine's inert form when Philip surged suddenly up from his throne. "By all the gods!" he cried, his face white, hands trembling. "This is not entertainment! This—this is obscene!"

Courtiers began murmuring all around the theater, but the players on stage paid none of this any notice. Pascal glanced over at Gabrielle, who had turned white as well, but with fright, not anger. Pascal raised his eyebrows in question, but the queen could only shrug helplessly in response.

Roe struggled on against the rising tide of audience disapproval. "He planted the bloody knife and heart on the king's person, cleaned himself, and then searched the castle for the infant prince, so he could kill it as well."

"This will stop *now!*" Philip cried, flecks of spittle flying from his mouth. "We order it!"

As the man in black slinked offstage, the wet nurse reappeared, evidently very frightened, two dolls clutched tightly to her chest. "But the prince's nurse had witnessed everything from her hidden alcove, and she fled the castle with the young prince and her own son both, pausing only long enough to remove a ring from the dead king's finger, before—"

King Philip shook his fist in the air. "Bring him back, bitch! You bring that young whelp back!"

Then he drew the ceremonial pistol from his belt and advanced toward the stage.

And Pascal, dread contracting his stomach, suddenly realized what this hellish play was all about.

XV.

Bert, watching from the wings, tried to tear his eyes away from the stage, but he could not. *The Usurper* had always seemed a ghoulish work to him, but now it took on a nightmare immediacy that it never had in any rehearsal.

Guillaume, his voice trembling, valiantly continued his narration as the real king, Philip the Good, approached the stage, pistol in hand, and as courtiers cried out scrambled to the edges of the theater. "So at last, frustrated in his in-in-inability to locate the prince," Guillaume read, "the advisor summoned to citizens of the village below to come in a witness the ghastly scene. Amazed as they were, their immediate thought—"

"We said stop!" Philip cried, as more actors rushed onto the stage, took in the scene, and hustled the groggy Jacques to his feet. One carried a rope, and as the advisor, his dark outer garments shed to reveal white clothes underneath, settled himself unobtrusively into the mock throne, the villagers fitted a noose about Paine's neck. "By all the gods above and all the demons below, we order you to desist from this obscenity! We will brook no disobedience!"

Bert wanted desperately to turn away, but the king's blood-red face held his attention and would let it go. Bert felt the beginnings of nausea as the players pantomimed Jacques's hanging, and as Philip mounted the stage.

"This ends now!" the king cried, leveling his pistol at Jacques.

Bert could tell that most everyone on stage wanted to run, to hide—the terror was etched that clearly on their faces—but they did not.

Jacques himself only raised tear-filled eyes to the vaulted ceiling and smiled sadly. "Oh, how I hope you'll forgive me for my foolishness, my dearest queen," he said, speaking the play's only line of dialogue. "I'll be with you soon."

And Philip the Good shot him in the center of the chest.

Blood—real blood—poured down the frilly blousing at the front of Jacques's doublet. Several people in the audience screamed, and Bert barely caught himself before crying out also.

"Do you hear me, Gérard?" Philip cried. "This ends now!"

But Jacques, the noose still tied around his neck, did not fall. Instead, he began the bobbing, weaving dance that was meant to simulate the dangling death throes of a hanging victim.

Philip cocked his pistol again. "Now!"

And he shot Jacques again.

Jacques stumbled but did not fall. He looked directly at the king as the dance continued, and he smiled.

"E-e-even as the new king wreaked atrocities in the kingdom newly fallen into his hands," Guillaume read, "the nurse had spirited the two boys away to a far country, where—"

"This ends, we said!" Philip exclaimed, tearing his eyes away from Jacques's bloody dance and crossing to where Guillaume stood. Shouts and cries filled the theater as the courtiers crowded the exits, none willing to witness what was happening. Philip raised the pistol again.

From where Bert stood, he could see Guillaume stiffen, but he could only imagine the look of fear in the man's eyes. "—wh-where she raised them to their youth and called them both her sons—Rene and—and—"

Philip fired, directly into Guillaume's face.

Guillaume rocked, and blood spattered the cornices that framed the stage.

"—and Jacques," Guillaume finished, his voice issuing hoarsely and wetly from the bloody maw that had been his nose and mouth. He also did not fall. "She—she raised them to be good men, but never let them for—*forget* the crimes she had witnessed in their former home of Montravel."

Bert fell to his knees, retching. These were not the words that had been rehearsed. None of the characters had names, and neither did the kingdom. He felt suffocated. He needed to save his people, but he could not move.

Terror roared like the pounding of a stampede of wild horses in his ears.

Rene and Emile, playing the two young foster brothers, had entered the stage from the opposite wings, and they spoke to a small knot of followers as Claude, in the rôle of the advisor, wreaked atrocities on his subjects on the near side of the stage.

"As the brothers grew," Guillaume recited, blood pumping onto the pages in his hand, "they hired trustworthy men to spy in Montravel, that they would know for themselves the sorry and indecent state of affairs—"

"Silence!" Philip roared, emptying the pistol into Guillaume's face and chest, until the hammer clicked on a hollow chamber.

". . . of affairs," Guillaume continued, swaying, "in . . . in the usurped . . . and cursed . . . land . . ."

An intricate dance ensued, spies crossing from one side of the stage to another, Emile and Rene hearing their reports, Claude and his wizard Auguste torturing their subjects and ravaging their land, as all the while Jacques bobbed and weaved like a bloody warning sign on the border between.

Philip backed slowly away from Guillaume, who continued his ghastly narrative. As he took in the frenzied scene around him, he hollered, "Guards! Kill these men! Every last one!"

And when no one heeded his call, Philip tossed away his pistol, drew his dagger, and hacked and slashed at the players as they danced helplessly past him.

When Bert saw Emile's throat cut, he rolled over, closed his eyes, and gagged.

Me, he thought. Kill me instead. Not them.

"Oh, God," he moaned. "Oh, my dear sweet God."

But Philip came nowhere near the wings. He left Bert completely alone.

XVI.

PASCAL ROSE SLOWLY TO HIS FEET, TREMBLING, DISBELIEVING the bloody spectacle before his eyes.

All but a hardy few courtiers had escaped the theater. Even most of the guards were missing. And on stage, the danse macabre went on, bodies continuing to cavort blindly even as Philip slashed at them mercilessly, even as their blood pumped out onto the stage, even as the music continued and they never stopped smiling.

"Die!" Philip cried, spinning and cutting. "Why will you damned souls not *die?*"

Pascal's throat tightened. The magic here was strong, but he had never guessed . . .

A whimper to his right at last caused Pascal to turn away from the horrific scene.

Gabrielle.

She was standing also, before her throne, shaking like the last leaf of autumn.

Pascal rushed to her, gathered her into his arms, and spun her away from the spectacle. "Oh, my dear, dear queen," he said, tears spilling over into his voice. "You should not see this."

She clung to him tightly, and as her whimpers subsided, Pascal glanced feverishly around the audience. Several ministers of state, high knights, clergymen, and a few guards still remained, but they were all rooted in place, mute, unable to look away from the stage.

"Can you watch and suffer this?" Pascal shouted at them, whirling with Queen Gabrielle still tight in his arms. His throat grew hot and raw. "Can all you great ones truly stand by and suffer this to continue? Can you?"

Their eyes all turned toward him.

"Well?" Pascal cried. The queen sobbed against him. "You've seen the evil here as plainly as I have. We've all been watching it for years, for decades, and now that it's heaped up around it like dung, are we all so inured to it that we can stand by and *watch?*"

And the most senior of the ministers, Lord Vincenzy, said, "Are you?"

And Pascal felt suddenly as if he had been struck in the stomach.

"No," he whispered hoarsely. "No, I cannot."

Stroking Gabrielle's hair, he lowered her gently into her throne.

"I'm sorry, Highness," he said, kneeling before her, "but now I *must* ask you to witness this. This is a lesson you will have to remember." He stood and surveyed the theater. "One we will *all* have to remember, for all the days of our lives. We are the strong ones, we who remain, and it is our *duty* to watch and remember, and to teach this lesson to everyone who was not strong enough to bear it today."

Pascal looked down at the queen, pale and trembling on her throne, and said, "Your Highness. Again, forgive me."

Then he turned and strode down the aisle.

Philip, weary and defeated, had sunk to his knees before the merrily cavorting bodies, his face buried in his bloody hands. Blood stained everything—the king's face, his robes, the players, the scenery. Blood ran across the stone floor in sheets, dripped in ragged curtains off the front of the stage. Blood had fallen into the glowing braziers, sending the raw scent of cooking flesh into the air.

Pascal swallowed down the bile rising in his throat and climbed onto the stage.

He nearly slipped in the blood as he rose to his feet. His flesh crawled as the gored bodies slowed in their dance, as the music stopped, as they gathered silently around him, twelve in all.

Philip's back was to Pascal. Pascal walked carefully to the king, mindful of his footing, then placed a hand on Philip's matted head.

The king started, looking up at Pascal with blue eyes that stared wildly from a face caked in blood. Philip held out his crimson hands.

"Pascal," he croaked, all arrogance banished from his voice. "Good Pascal. Sweet Pascal. Help me, Pascal. My—my hands . . ."

Pascal swallowed. "Yes, your hands, Majesty," he said softly. "They seem to be stained."

Philip's gaze slowly traveled around the circle of bloody bodies, then back to Pascal. "All this . . ."

Pascal looked up, met the staring eyes of each player in turn. Their crimson-on-bone faces, their pain-filled eyes, their sweet smiles—those with smiles still intact—all seemed to beg him for release.

He stared into Jacques Paine's eyes last of all. The wig had fallen from Paine's head, and clotting blood now obscured the gray streaks in his beard. Two balls of lead and countless thrusts of Philip's dagger had pierced his chest, but otherwise Paine's body was unmarked.

"Your Majesty," Pascal said, bowing to King Jacques, Montravel's rightful ruler.

"I . . ." King Jacques coughed up bloody foam as he tried to form the words. His voice frothed and bubbled. "I . . . I . . . I believe you know the—the protocol better than I."

"Yes, Majesty," Pascal said, turning his gaze back down to Philip, who knelt in the living blood of a dozen good men. Pascal had hoped to use Philip at the focus of the Lens, for the restoration of the kingdom, but he realized now that this was impossible. This usurper had long ago drained himself dry of all but the most vestigial goodness, and he had nothing of value left to give to Montravel.

If Pascal used Philip as he had planned, it would only poison the kingdom further.

"I accuse you, Philip Théophile," Pascal said, his hand still in the usurper's hair. "I accuse you of the heinous murder of the rightful monarch of Montravel over thirty years, and of the subsequent weakening and devastation of Montravel."

"But, Pascal," Philip said, smiling weakly, spreading his hands, "I only—"

"Silence," Pascal said, smoothing Philip's hair. He fought the quaver in his voice. "I also accuse you of the untimely deaths of more of your subjects than you could possibly count, and with the—" His voice cracked, and he looked around the circle again.

Jacques Paine nodded.

"And with the murders of these twelve good men, whose only crime was a love of order and justice."

Now Pascal nodded to Paine, who raised a pale, dripping arm and pointed at Philip. "I accuse you, Philip Théophile."

And, each in turn, every other member of the circle pointed to the usurper and repeated the words: "I accuse you, Philip Théophile."

Philip's head trembled beneath Pascal's hand. He whimpered silently.

Pascal addressed the sparse audience. "Is there anyone here who would disagree with a judgment of guilt?"

No one spoke. No one moved.

"Then I pronounce you guilty, Philip Théophile," Pascal said. "I pronounce you guilty of all the above crimes, and of all others for which you may yet nurture secret responsibility." At that point, Pascal looked out at Gabrielle, who sat very still in her throne, tears sparkling like diamonds on her cheeks. "The penalty for these crimes is death, and there is no appeal."

Pascal bent to retrieve Philip's dagger, which had fallen to the floor. The haft and blade both were sticky with blood.

"The sentence of death may only be executed by the sitting king himself, or by his designee," Pascal said. "Will you execute the sentence yourself, Philip?"

Philip's eyebrows drew together in a puzzled knot. "What? You would have me . . . ?"

Pascal closed his eyes and drew a deep breath. This was the last thing he wanted to do—but only because he had wanted so desperately to do it for so long.

"I will take that as declining," he said. "And as chief advisor—not that my capacity was ever respected—I take myself as the designee by default."

And in one swift motion, Pascal pulled Philip's head back sharply by the hair and drew the bloody dagger across his throat.

A hot gout of blood sprayed across Pascal's thighs, and he instantly released both Philip and the blade. Philip's hands curled into shaking claws, waving ineffectually in the air as the life and breath gurgled out of him.

All around Pascal, expressions of contentment settled on the faces of the twelve players, and one by one they slumped to the floor.

Jacques Paine was the last to go. "It . . . is finished," he said, then released a great shuddering breath and collapsed.

Pascal stood frozen for several moments in the midst of all the blood and all the bodies. He held his own hands up before his eyes, staring at them in wonderment. The theater was silent, and it was only after a dozen hushed breaths that he realized the remaining nobles were waiting for him to speak.

"Remember this, friends," Pascal said, words nearly failing him. "Remember what you have seen, and remember that this is not the end of Montravel's difficulties. It is only the start. For one thing, we are kingless."

Then Gabrielle stood, smoothing her spotless gown. "Why can you not take his place?"

A warmth from deep inside him crawled slowly to the front of his eyes and spilled. "Ah, Your Highness, I fall well outside the proper chain of succession—and besides, I have other work to do." He looked down at the bloody floor. "Work that only I can do."

"But then who else?" Lord Vincenzy said. "The proper heir to the throne is dead, Philip left no issue, and Montravel's charter demands a patriarchal succession."

And that was when Bert Dram meekly emerged from the backstage shadows, wringing his hands in clear agitation.

"Um," he said, "I have something you might want to see."

XVII.

WHILE THE MAGICIAN PASCAL DEMAIN EXAMINED THE SILVER signet ring, Bert knelt beside the bodies of his friends, the men he had worked beside and loved for so long. He smoothed Guillaume's hair, stroked Claude's arm, touched poor young Emile's cheek. He nodded gravely to Rene's staring face, then moved to Jacques.

Jacques, who had been like a captain to Bert—a captain, a best friend, even a son.

Bert dragged the body up into a sitting position, heedless of all the people watching, and clasped it to his chest. "Oh, Jacques," he said, blinking rapidly even though he had no tears left to shed. "I knew you for so long, and I still didn't know you at all. I didn't know you at all."

Lord Vincenzy and Queen Gabrielle had joined Pascal on stage, and they all huddled together over the ring Bert had produced. "This is certainly the signet," Pascal said. "At least, it matches all the drawings I've seen. You say Jacques gave it to you?"

Bert nodded forlornly, cradling Jacques's body. "Just before the show started. He told me if—" He felt himself losing control, and fought to regain it. "He told me if anything were to happen to him, that I should take his place. Of course, no one could take his place. There's no one . . ."

"Do you think that satisfies the charter, Vincenzy?" Pascal asked.

The minister raised his eyebrows. "As far as I understand it."

As the eyes of the three nobles turned toward him, Bert began shaking his head uneasily. "No, no, I gave it to you, milord. It's yours. Take it."

The magician breathed heavily, glancing sideways at the queen. "Jacques praised you very highly this evening, where I would be certain to take notice. I think he had this in mind all along. Don't you?"

Bert lowered his head. He knew what Jacques had in mind—there could be no mistaking it now—but he did not understand it. He did not understand it at all. "Why, Jacques?" he asked the dead man in his arms. "Why me?"

The magician returned to where Bert sat, lifted one of Bert's unresisting hands, and slipped the ring onto his index finger. "We may yet find that out . . . Your Majesty. I'm betting we will."

Then everyone in the theater knelt and bowed toward him, and Bert could only blink uncomprehendingly and clutch the Jacques's body more tightly to his chest.

XVIII.

As Vincenzy and the other lords conferred with Bert Dram, Pascal drew Gabrielle aside.

"Oh, Pascal," she said as he led her to a far dim corner of the theater, "I can't believe all this has really happened."

Pascal, a heavy stone weighing on his heart, could not look her in the eyes. "And yet it has, Your Highness."

Gabrielle drew toward him, cupping his face in her hands. Her clear gray eyes were sparkling and bright, though the traces of great pain still lingered. Her smile was tentative, yet radiant. "No, no more titles. I'm stepping down as queen, Pascal. With Philip dead, I have no claim on the throne, and we can finally be together."

Pascal embraced her tightly then, staring out over the top of her soft, soft hair toward the bloody tableau on the stage. "No, Gabrielle," he said. "No, we can't."

She pulled away suddenly, looking up at him in concern. "Why—what do you mean? Of course we can. There's nothing to stop us now."

Tears filled Pascal's eyes, and he had to blink them away.

"Yes, there is. I told you I had important work to do, work that only I could do." He looked down at her, so lovely in the torch-light, so delicate, so strong. "It probably means my life—but then, how can I do any less for Montravel than I've seen done here today?"

"But, Pascal . . ."

"Shh," he said, then bent to kiss her. Her lips were warm and smooth, and she wrapped her arms around him tightly.

He did not want the moment to end.

Finally, though, he drew away from her, pulled out a fresh handkerchief from his pocket and brushed the tears from her face. Her gown had been clean and white before they kissed—except for the hem that had trailed through the blood on the stage—but now dull red stains marked the places where their bodies had touched.

"Goodbye, Gabrielle," he said, then kissed her forehead and walked away.

He slipped out of the theater unnoticed, then down a concealed stairway to the door that led into the very heart of the Keep. To where the Lens was housed.

Pascal hoped he was a good enough man to undo what Donatien and Philip had done to Montravel.

As he touched the lock to spell it open, he heard a soft tread on the stair behind him. Very little torchlight filtered down, but he could still see her well enough to recognize her.

"Gabrielle . . ." He stopped, at a loss for wards.

She drew closer. "Whatever this is you need to do . . . are you sure can't use any help?"

"It means draining myself of my life energy, very slowly over a very long period of time. It won't be very pleasant."

Gabrielle smoothed her bloody gown, looking at the floor.

"No—but I still don't understand why we couldn't do it together. If it's that important . . ."

Pascal looked into the shadows for a long, long time. He fought to suppress the yearning in his heart, but it was futile.

"If this is what you really want, then I suppose it's wrong of me to try to stop you," he said. "But it will be the hardest thing either of us has ever done."

Gabrielle rushed to him, embraced him. "I'm ready," she said, and Pascal slipped his arm around her.

Together, they entered the chamber.

XIX.

GENTLY, BERT LOWERED JACQUES'S BODY TO THE FLOOR. HE closed the staring eyes, kissed each lid, and then let Lord Vincenzy help him back to his feet.

He took a deep breath, willing away the tremor in his voice. "There's a lot I need to learn, gentlemen," he said. "And I'm willing to start any time you are."

If this was truly what Jacques wanted, then Bert would serve to the best of his abilities.

It was the very least that he could do.

www.ingramcontent.com/pod-product-compliance
Lightning Source LLC
Chambersburg PA
CBHW022042170626
46808CB00003B/1336